A Frog in the Bog

To my wonderful agent, Steve, who helped me make it in the frog-eat-bug world of writing
—K. W.

For Lana and Chris. In memory of your childhood
—J. R.

ISBN 0-439-69726-3

Text copyright © 2003 by Karma Wilson.
Illustrations copyright © 2003 by Joan Rankin. All rights reserved.
Published by Scholastic Inc., 557 Broadway, New York, NY 10012, by arrangement with Margaret K. McElderry Books, Simon & Schuster Children's Publishing Division.
SCHOLASTIC and associated logos are trademarks and/or registered trademarks of Scholastic Inc.

12 11 10 9 8 7 6 5 4 3 2 1   4 5 6 7 8 9/0

Printed in the U.S.A.   40

First Scholastic printing, November 2004

Book design by Kristin Smith
The text for this book is set in Gorilla.
The illustrations for this book are rendered in watercolor.

karma wilson

joan rankin

A Frog in the Bog

SCHOLASTIC INC.
NEW YORK TORONTO LONDON AUCKLAND SYDNEY
MEXICO CITY NEW DELHI HONG KONG BUENOS AIRES

There's a frog on the log in the middle of the bog.

A small, green frog
on a half-sunk log
in the middle of the bog.

He flicks ONE tick
as it creeps up a stick.

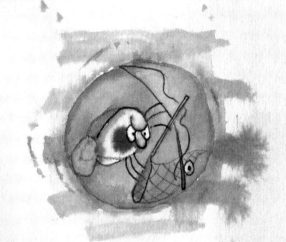

ONE tick in the belly of a small, green frog
on a half-sunk log
in the middle of the bog.

And the frog grows
a little bit
bigger. . . .

He sees TWO fleas
as they leap through the reeds.

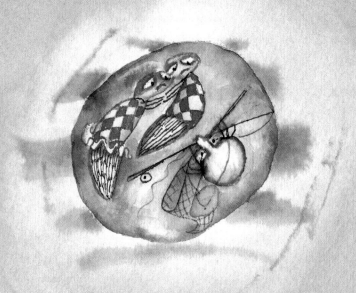

ONE tick, TWO fleas
in the belly of the frog
on a half-sunk log
in the middle of the bog.

And the frog grows
a little bit
bigger. . . .

He spies THREE flies
as they buzz through the skies.

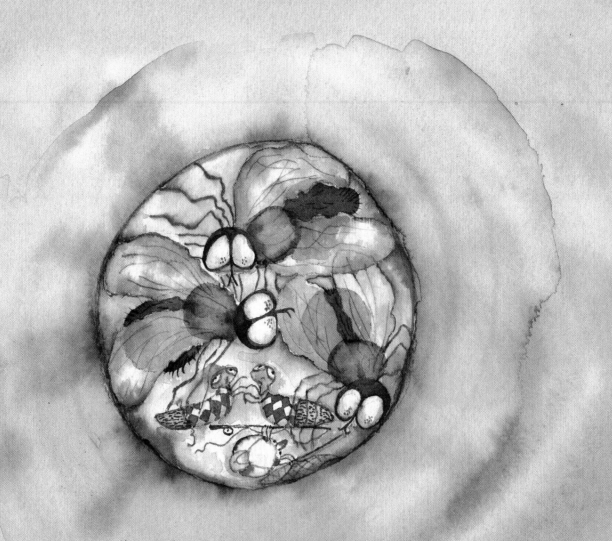

ONE tick, **TWO** fleas, **THREE** flies (Oh, my!)
in the belly of the frog
on a half-sunk log
in the middle of the bog.

And the frog grows
a little bit
bigger. . . .

He glugs FOUR slugs
as they slink through the sludge.

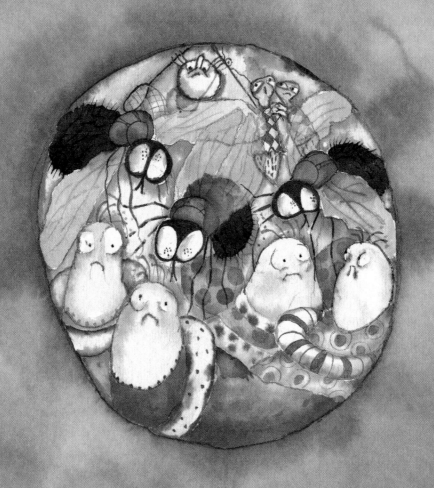

ONE tick, TWO fleas, THREE flies (Oh, my!),
FOUR slugs (Ew, ugh!) in the belly of the frog
on a half-sunk log
in the middle of the bog.

And the frog grows
a little bit
bigger. . . .

He inhales FIVE snails
from their heads to their tails!

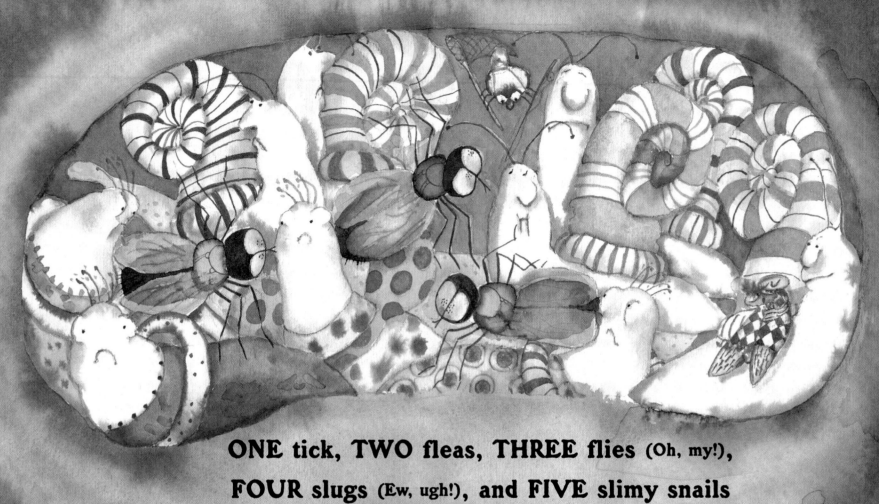

ONE tick, TWO fleas, THREE flies (Oh, my!),
FOUR slugs (Ew, ugh!), and FIVE slimy snails
in the belly of the frog
on a half-sunk log
in the middle of the bog.

What a hog, that frog!

And the frog grows
a little bit
bigger!!!

Then . . .

that log with the frog
in the middle of the bog
starts to rise . . .

and the frog sees eyes!

And the frog sees claws
and a big set of jaws,
and a mouth like a crater!
And the frog screams,

With his mouth open wide,
all the bugs inside
start to crawl and fly
and to slither and slide.

Out come FIVE snails
from their heads to their tails,

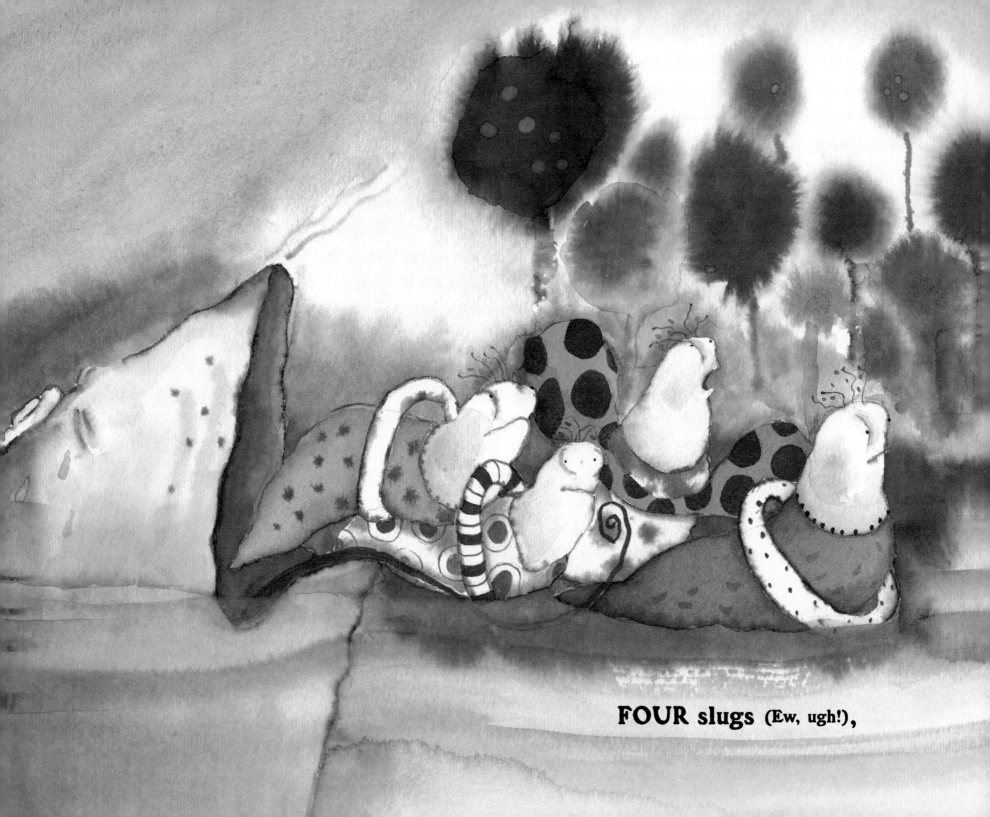

FOUR slugs (Ew, ugh!),

TWO fleas (Dear me!),

and ONE tiny tick.

ICK!

And right in the middle of his holler,

that frog grows
a whole lot
smaller. . . .

"See ya later," says the gator
as he romps through the swamp,
cuz the itty-bitty frog
isn't big enough to chomp.

Now . . .

the bugs in the bog
keep away from the frog,

and the frog NEVER sits on a half-sunk log!